I0761440

UNCLE PATRICK'S SECESSIONIST BREAKFAST

McSWEENEY'S
SAN FRANCISCO

This is the eighth in a series of stories that will, god willing, someday become something larger, called *The Forgetters*.

Originally published in the *San Francisco Chronicle*.

Cover illustration by Annie Dills.

ISBN: 978-1-963270-43-3

These numbers could mean anything, or nothing:
10 9 8 7 6 5 4 3 2 1

www.mcsweeneys.net

Printed in Canada

UNCLE PATRICK'S SECESSIONIST BREAKFAST

by

DAVE EGGERS

McSWEENEY'S

To JB

THE DAY was cool and the sky a satin white. Edie was hustling around the courtyard carrying folding chairs and coffee cups. No one was helping.

The night before had been more than anyone wanted. It was the first night of the Mahoney reunion and the tweens had driven the ATV into a ditch. Cousin Aurora, a Monterey whale-watching captain, had gotten tipsy early on Oisín's bathtub gin and had broken a chandelier while trying to change one of the bulbs. Shards of it were still being found all over the kitchen and TV room of the main house. Aurora was still in bed, afraid to be seen.

By midmorning Patrick, the patriarch, was up and insisting that everyone come to the courtyard. He and Edie had set up a dozen mismatched chairs in the shade of three badly bent lemon trees. The Mahoney family reunion, Patrick's idea, had been hitched to his eighty-second birthday, with Edie, his middle daughter, doing most of the planning. As she always did.

Maeve, Patrick's wife and Edie's mother, had been in charge for half a century. She'd passed on one warm night in September and Edie and her kids had moved onto the property to watch over it and Patrick. The main house was a chalky and falling-down Spanish colonial sitting on a hundred and thirty-four rolling acres on California's Central Coast. Tucked into the straw-colored hills were a half-dozen crooked outbuildings, and a man-made lake, and a pile of rusted metal that had once been a WWI biplane. The land had been used for cattle grazing for a hundred years, but when Patrick turned eighty he let Edie sell the cows and plant fruit.

"I'm setting out the strawberry lemonade," Edie said, "and the kids are gathering some fruit and there should be some good bread coming. Oh here it is. Thank you Lori."

Lori, her younger sister, was fifty-four, an immigration lawyer in San Jose. She'd sliced two loaves of

French bread and set it on the pizza oven Cole had built, which had never worked. No one had the heart to tell Cole, but in the meantime it made a very good staging site for the refreshments.

"Serve yourselves," Edie said. "We know how Oisín feels about being waited on."

Oisín, Patrick's younger brother at seventy-eight, lived in Idaho and had a thing about restaurants, waiters and anyone acting like a waiter. He refused to be served and liked to talk about why. At the moment, though, Oisín was sitting on a stiff wooden chair, his body a perfect forty-five-degree angle, his arms crossed over his chest. His hair was long and white, his nose narrow and broken, and with his sunglasses on, it was impossible to know whether he was judging or napping.

The night before had gone late, and Patrick and Edie had pushed the morning event back an hour to accommodate hangovers and jetlag. By eleven, the marine layer had burned off and the sun was high and bright. The guest speakers were ready, sitting side by side on two wingback chairs that Edie and her baby brother Cole had dragged out of the living room.

"I don't ask much of you all," Patrick said to the twelve Mahoneys gathered. Beyond Patrick's kids, there was a smattering of their spouses and cousins, and everyone felt sure this symposium would be stultifying. "I've never asked you to listen to a lecture or fireside chat before," Patrick said. "But I ask you to indulge me and listen to our guests. I saw them speak at the library in Gilroy and was very impressed. They kindly agreed to come speak to our gathering, so I expect manners and engagement. Let the record show, Calla, that I don't approve of your T-shirt."

Lori's daughter Calla was wearing a homemade shirt that said, simply, GENITALS. A willowy eighteen-year-old with a mop of curly blond hair, she'd recently been suspended for listing her high school for sale on Craigslist. She was so clever, and her pranks had such wit, that no one worried much about her. Sitting on a tilting beach chair, she gave her grandfather a professional nod. She apparently had no regrets.

"Anyway," Patrick continued, "this is Franklin Ghent… Wait. Is it 'Gent' like 'gentleman,' or Ghent like Belgian Ghent?"

"Ghent like Belgium," Franklin said. Franklin was shaped like a refrigerator box, with bright pink skin and a neatly trimmed white beard. He wore red-rimmed glasses, jeans with suspenders, and a crisp pale-blue button-down. He seemed very at ease, very content, delighted to be surrounded by people and food, like a happy mall Santa.

"Good," Patrick said. "And this is Daniel Chavez. They're from the California Independence Coalition. I think what they're proposing makes at least as much sense as the current situation, which is, in a few words, illogical and stupid. So Daniel and Franklin, take it away."

Daniel was taller, leaner, with a sharper look—dark bright eyes, assessing eyebrows, a V-shaped chin. He was wearing a plum-colored T-shirt and black basketball shorts. He stood and swept his eyes across the attendees and smiled stiffly. "I want to first say that I'm sorry I'm wearing shorts. I saw the forecast and thought it would be about a hundred degrees down here. I'm from Concord, so…"

No one was quite sure what being from Concord had to do with the temperature and his shorts.

"Don't worry for a second," Patrick said. "We're not a formal group. Look at Oisín here. He's had those shoes since 1981. And he might be asleep."

Oisín did not stir.

Edie looked at Oisín and winced. Whenever they had company like this—people who had never been to the property, had never met the family—she was struck by how odd they surely seemed to outsiders. There was a bathtub visible in the meadow below the main house, and in the tub someone had put the upper half of a mannequin. That must have happened last night; the model and its unblinking stare hadn't been there the day before. The main house was behind a wide dirt and gravel roundabout, built for stagecoaches and now crowded with cars and trucks and the petals of a series of cherry blossom trees that no one could remember planting.

"Wait," Edie said. "Sorry. I should have given you guys some lemonade. Hold on." She got up, which provoked a groan from her son Torin. Everyone knew Edie didn't like to sit still. Tanned and lean and wearing baggy jeans and cloth tennis shoes, she poured Daniel and Franklin strawberry lemonade. Theirs were the only two glasses that matched. Edie and Patrick were alike in that neither saw the point in matching sets of anything.

"The kids and I made it this morning," she said. "All grown here." Ghent and Chavez glanced at the lemon trees immediately behind them and smiled.

"Oh, not those," Edie said. "Those don't produce anything good. The best ones are over there." She pointed beyond the main house and beyond the half-burned gray barn, to a parched mohair hill where a necklace of florid green trees stood. The lemons that dotted the trees looked like dollops of yellow paint straight from the jar.

"Even better," Franklin said. "Have you all been on this land a long time?"

"Is two hundred years a long time?" Patrick said.

Edie sat down. "It hasn't been two hundred years, Dad. We got here in 1855."

"Our people bought this parcel off the Spanish," Patrick explained. "It's been mostly cattle land until a few years ago. I retired and then Edie filled it with bizarre fruit trees."

"*Exotics*, Dad," Edie said, and got up again, headed back toward the house.

“Edie please sit,” Patrick said, but she was gone, under the hummingbird feeder and around the hedge. “Sorry. You guys can start.”

Daniel stood up. “Should we wait for…?” he asked.

“Edie? No,” Patrick said.

“Well, thank you, Patrick,” Daniel said. “We’re very honored to be here, and we believe this couldn’t be a more important moment in our state’s history…” he smiled, and seemed, for an inordinately long time, to lose his power of speech. It was clear that he was scanning the group for Katherine Sarver, Patrick and Maeve’s eldest daughter. She’d been a two-term senator from California and was now three years into restless retirement. Katherine was somewhere in the main house, or out hiking; she’d let Edie know that she didn’t want to be within ten miles of these crackpots.

“Katherine’s not here. Did you want her here?” Lori said, a shade of mocking in her voice. Of course Franklin and Daniel wanted the former senator there. Lori had been the most vocal about her displeasure with the morning’s program. Shorter and feistier than her sisters, Lori was an unceasingly pragmatic

Democrat who'd run her sister Katherine's first campaign and loathed impractical idealogues from either side.

"Not a problem!" Daniel said. "I don't know how the former senator feels about the topic, but—"

"How does a former senator of the United States feel about its most populous state seceding?" Lori said.

"Keep your mind open, Lore," Patrick said. "They haven't even started yet."

"The rest of us are listening," Edie said, rushing back to the scene with a plate of scones. She was eyeing Oisín, who still had not stirred.

"Well," Daniel said, "as Patrick noted, we're from the California Independence Coalition. I'm the chief strategist, and Franklin is the director of research and policy. As you probably inferred, we're in favor of California either seceding to become an independent nation, or somehow attaining a degree of autonomy that would have all the benefits of nationhood."

"More than any other time in California's history," Franklin said, "it's clear we want drastically different things from most of the rest of this country. California's approach to immigration is different. Our environmental standards are decades ahead of most of the country. We respect a woman's right to choose and value diversity and overwhelmingly want single-payer health care. We're like a rocket ship that could do and see the most extraordinary things, but we're held back by carrying the deadweight of regressive states and their regressive policies."

Daniel jumped in. "Right now our role in this country's fortunes is untenable. We provide more to the federal coffers than any other state, and yet our votes have not counted in a presidential election since 1876. We are drastically underrepresented in Congress, a body that is determined to retreat into the past, while California has always been a forward-looking place."

He looked to Franklin, who was sipping his strawberry lemonade. Franklin took the cue. He released the glass from his mouth, but a filament of spittle stretched between the two and took an agonizingly long time to give up.

"On every issue," Franklin said, unaware that a dozen people had just seen what they'd seen, "California is held in the past by a regressive

Republican base. The cold truth is that the issues you're seeing with Trump, these are Civil War issues. The majority of his voters are poorly educated whites, the same people who fought the Union one hundred and sixty years ago. And in most ways they haven't changed much. Meanwhile, twenty-seven percent of California is foreign-born. This is a state that respects diversity. It's in large part why we're the biggest and richest state."

"California has had more Nobel winners in the last ten years than the South has had in the history of the nation," Daniel noted. "This is a state that's open to innovation. Some of these Trump states, not too much."

"It's like someone from 2025 married to someone from 1889," Franklin said. "Naturally, no one's happy."

"That's a good line," Oisín said. "You two write that?"

"He speaks!" Patrick cried. Oisín still hadn't moved.

"Now, you may be wondering how a single state could become its own nation," Daniel said. "Our belief is that in most ways, we already *are* a separate nation.

And we certainly have the resources to act as one. In 2022 our GDP was $3.64 trillion—the fifth-largest economy in the world..."

"I thought it was sixth," Cole said.

Lori turned to her little brother and assessed him. Cole was forty-two, dark haired and soft shouldered and open to any and all alternative histories of UFOs, the building of the pyramids and the origin of Covid. Every few years he reshaped himself, without fanfare, into some new career. He'd been in IT, then sold solar panels, then was a fish broker, and most recently worked for a company that built panic rooms. Of all the family members in attendance, he was the most likely to have voted for Jill Stein. Lori could not speak, ever again, to anyone who had voted for Jill Stein, so was determined to never ask him.

"It varies," Franklin clarified. "Sometimes we're bigger than England, sometimes they're bigger than us."

"And we have forty million people," Franklin said, "about one-eighth of the U.S. population. But because of the Electoral College, our votes are almost meaningless."

"I once voted for Gary Cooper," Oisín said. "I wrote him in second time Nixon ran."

"Was he still alive?" Patrick asked.

"Not sure," Oisín said.

"Remember when Carrot Top ran for governor?" Edie asked Calla.

"Who's Carrot Top?" Calla asked.

"Focus, people," Patrick implored.

"The point is," Daniel said, "we're a net giver into the federal economy. We put in $2.5 trillion, and we get out $350 billion."

"And we have proportionally little power in Congress," Franklin said. "We have one senator for every twenty million people. Wyoming, on the other hand, has one for every three hundred thousand. The same disconnect holds in the House."

"The rural states are overwhelmingly white," Daniel added, "and they have wildly disproportionate power in Congress and the Electoral College."

"Which was by design," Oisín noted.

"And still they make fun of us," Cole said.

"They hate us," Edie said. "Or pretend to hate us. Then they come to Universal Studios."

"What about the vulnerable in these red states?" Lori asked. "Who protects them?"

"You're saying California currently protects, say, the undocumented in West Virginia?" Patrick asked. "And yes, I know you're a lawyer."

"The vulnerable elsewhere could move here," Franklin said. "You'd have the largest population realignment since WWII. Oh, who's this?"

Paolo, Edie's five-year-old, had appeared at Franklin's side, carrying an armful of unusual fruit. "Oh, don't do that, Paolo," Edie said, striding toward him. But Paolo had already dumped the fruit in Franklin's lap.

"Okay! What do we have here?" Franklin asked.

"That's a lychee," Paolo said. "That's a dragon fruit."

"The kid knows his fruit," Daniel said, and reached for a strange cucumber still in Paolo's hand. "Do I get some?" he asked, but Paolo didn't acknowledge him. He'd chosen Santa.

Franklin didn't know what to do about the fruit in his lap. Smiling politely, he moved them, one by one, to the stone deck next to his chair.

A phone began ringing. Pockets were checked. Franklin and Daniel smiled serenely.

"Dad, that's yours, I think," Edie said. Patrick looked at his own pocket for a long time, as if disappointed in the audacity of the phone within. He took it out and looked at the number. "It's Wes calling from Boston." He pushed the red button to send his nephew to voicemail.

"I'll call back later," Patrick said. "There's always more time in California."

Groans sounded from all quarters. Patrick had been saying this for decades. When the East Coast was going to sleep, he'd say, California had three more hours. When the Midwest was huddled inside, sequestered by snow, California had months of sun. "Always more here—more land, more sun, more time," he'd say.

"Let's talk about taxes," Franklin said. "Right now, we pay more than any other state. You have the federal income tax, then you have our state's progressive income tax, which tops out at about twelve percent for the wealthiest. I'm guessing some of you pay twenty-five percent or more to DC. Then another ten or so to Sacramento..."

"Between the two, I'm at forty-four percent," Patrick said, and Oisín's head fell forward. He lowered his sunglasses to look at his brother.

"Well, imagine that federal tax is gone," Franklin continued. "If California becomes its own nation, you'd only pay one tax, and we'd make it a progressive one, and very reasonable. If the billionaires who live here paid their share, even at twenty or thirty percent we'd have more than enough revenue to fund everything—health care, Head Start, daycare, infrastructure, firefighting, gun control, schools. Remember that $2.5 trillion that now stays in California? We could make every UC free to every student forever."

"And this becomes a draw for businesses. Same thing—one tax rate instead of two," Daniel said.

"That's major," Cole said.

"And imagine they're free from the absurdity of covering their employees' health insurance," Franklin said. "Remember that we're the only country in the industrialized world operating under that absurd system. Why is a snack shop involved in an employee's cancer treatment? The rest of the world—their jaws are on the ground when we try to explain our health care system."

"There's no way to explain it," Edie said.

"With single-payer," Daniel said, "all the inexcusable waste in the health care system floats away. And again, billions saved that we can spend more wisely."

Franklin was looking for something in his valise but didn't find it. "I had a chart..." he mumbled, then looked up brightly. "Anyway, between health care, the best schools, and a lower overall tax rate, we'd instantly become the most appealing location in the world to do business."

"Huh," Oisín said, which from him was high praise.

Daniel opened his palms theatrically. "And can anyone think of anything we get from the federal government that we couldn't reproduce on our own?"

"Okay, I'll bite. What about the military?" Oisín said. Now his sunglasses were halfway down his nose. He seemed to be slowly acknowledging that he was awake and listening.

"Honestly, we wouldn't need one," Daniel said. "Not a significant one at least. We'd have the same kind of army that, say, Norway has. Functional but not adventuresome."

"Think of us like New Zealand," Franklin added. "That's a good corollary, in terms of our politics and way of life. Or Costa Rica. These countries are advanced and progressive, and decidedly peaceful."

"Think of Canada, too," Daniel said. "Trump says that Canada needs our military, but when was the last time Canada was invaded? Did I miss some Russian assault?"

"Hear that, teens? You wouldn't have to register for the draft," Patrick said.

Calla gave Patrick a fake smile. Torin, though, was lost in thought, picturing the explosion of the nearest star. A week ago, he'd seen a video that showed what would happen to Earth if the nearest star died a violent death. The blast would obliterate Earth, of course, but the thing that Torin couldn't get out of his mind was that it would take 4.3 years before the explosion reached Earth. Four years! Astronomers would know the instant this star exploded, but then we'd have 4.3 years to live, waiting and knowing. How strange that was! What would humanity do? What would *he* do?

For one thing, he wanted to spend more time with Calla. He was secretly and chastely in love with Calla.

"Hey," Calla said, and kicked his foot. He startled and his eyes focused and found her. "If I have to listen, you have to, too," she said.

"Okay. I was," he said.

"You weren't," she said.

After watching the video—just a brief animation made by some Danish graduate students—Torin hadn't been able to sleep. The thought of the 4.3 years came to him often throughout his nights and days, and had come to him now, while these two strange men were babbling about politics.

She kicked him again. "Hello? Are you high?"

"No," he said, and decided not to say, *I've never been high*. Though that was the truth. Torin was sixteen but had not smoked pot, and even if he did smoke pot, he was not the kind of person who would smoke pot in the morning, at a family reunion.

"I think you're high," she said.

"I'm not high," he said.

"Then pay attention," she said, and she turned toward the two men, who looked to Torin like an insufferable comedy duo from a black-and-white movie.

"What about the forty-six percent of the state owned by the feds?" Patrick asked.

"They own forty-six percent of California?" Calla asked.

"They do," Daniel said. "But we could buy it back. The federal government will need our money—the money they're not getting from our tax base—so they'll be happy to sell it."

"They won't be *happy* to sell it," Franklin corrected. "But they'd sell it."

"They can use the money to buy Greenland," Cole said, but no one laughed.

"What about China?" Calla asked. "Like in terms of being a threat?" Lori, her mom, winked at her and mouthed *Good question*.

"We don't believe that China would invade a sovereign Western nation," Franklin said. "It's never happened before. And we'd be a member of NATO and the UN, of course, so any such invasion is kind of unlikely. No offense." He winked at Calla, who looked to the hills.

"The main thing you'd need is border patrol," Daniel said. "But again, with the $2.5 trillion we're keeping, we could probably buy some boats and trucks."

"But what *would* the border policy be?" Lori asked.

"Finally!" Edie said. "I thought I was going to have to ask for you."

"That's TBD," Franklin said. "But it would be sane, and organized, and would reflect the state's multicultural history."

"Well, that tells me very little," Lori said.

"I should underline that we're not kings here," Franklin said. "We're suggesting a path that would make this state the most prosperous and progressive nation on Earth. But we'd be a democracy, and border policy would be determined by elected lawmakers."

"So we're sticking to bicameral, or something else?" Patrick asked.

"The simplest thing is to just use Sacramento as the capital of the new nation, with the legislative districts more or less the same," Daniel said. "Our personal view is that you'd retain whatever you could to ease the transition. And Sacramento currently functions pretty well."

Patrick coughed extravagantly but said nothing.

"Can't we get rid of the two-party system?" Calla asked. "If we're going full European and all."

"Other parties would definitely have more viability in a new nation," Franklin said. "Especially if we remove all private money from elections—which is my personal goal. Daniel is not as insistent, but I do think we might as well excise one of the central cancers festering within American democracy. No monetary donations would be allowed to any candidates, period. Elected officials would be prohibited from trading stocks while in office, and prohibited from becoming lobbyists after leaving office. Take all the money out, period. We all know it's the right choice, and it's only blindness and sloth that's gotten us to this point of maximum corruption."

"Again," Franklin said, "we'd be looking to Western Europe for inspiration on some of these things. We'd borrow the best practices from there and all over the world. While keeping all that we like about the U.S. Constitution of course."

"Well, I sorta like the whole idea," Edie said. "If nothing else, it's worth a try. We can't just sit around and watch the country implode."

This got Torin's attention. "I agree," he said, and Calla turned to him and smiled.

Lori's mouth fell open. "I can't believe you people."

Edie stared back at her little sister. "What? It's exciting," she said. She turned to Daniel and Franklin. "Seriously, can it actually be done?"

"I'll answer that," Lori said. "No way. The Constitution forbids it."

"Well," Franklin said, "it's not constitutionally *forbidden*. But the process would be challenging."

"We already tried this once," Lori said. "Remember 1861? Seems like there were some hiccups that time around."

"Lori, we're just listening here. No one's taking up muskets," Patrick said. "So guys, this is via referendum, I assume? Don't you need the cooperation of the rest of the states? Otherwise it's the Confederacy all over again."

"Good question. Thank you," Daniel said. "The first step would be a referendum on the state ballot.

We get six hundred thousand signatures, and the question can be voted on. If a majority of voters favor secession, we send those results to Congress."

"And they say go fuck yourselves," Lori said. She caught Calla's eye. "Sorry."

"Well, yes, Congress does need to sign off on the secession," Franklin said. "It has to be a mutual breakup. It would take a two-thirds vote in both houses of Congress, and would have to be ratified by thirty-eight states."

"I bet we could get thirty-eight," Patrick said. "That's basically Trump's Electoral College. Honestly, who would object?"

"The other blue states, dummy," Lori said. "We'd be leaving them high and dry."

"So if Congress votes against it, then what?" Edie asked.

"We'd still have a new kind of leverage," Franklin said. "The rest of the country would be on alert that on many fronts, we're going to do our own thing. I'm personally in favor of the state withholding federal tax revenue unless certain concessions are met."

"That's the Civil War again," Lori said.

"The governor of Maine proposed the same thing a month ago," Franklin said. "Things are going so far off the rails that it's time for more states' rights. The GOP can't argue with that."

"I think health care would be first," Daniel said. "We'd start single-payer the day after the referendum."

"And the Supreme Court shoots it down," Lori said.

"On what grounds?" Daniel asked.

Patrick looked to the house. "It'd be nice if Katherine were out here. She'd know."

Lori's neck veins went taut. "Kath doesn't run the Supreme Court, Dad. She barely practiced law." Her father shrugged.

"But let's say for the sake of argument that we no longer *are* bound by the Supreme Court," Daniel said. "Maybe as a function of our voters' will to secede, we say we'll stay in the Union, to some extent, but that court is no longer *our* court."

Lori scoffed loudly. "Insanity."

"The point is, there would be a balance of power," Daniel said. "The next time some congressman from

Mississippi threatens to withhold aid after a wildfire in our state, we can withhold the billions our citizens put into the federal coffers."

"Why not just focus on the Electoral College?" Lori asked. "If you get rid of that, most of these issues go away. California and New York would actually have the power of their populations."

"That means amending the Constitution," Franklin said. "And that takes a supermajority. Do you know twenty Republican senators and a hundred congressmen who would willingly vote to decrease their own influence?"

"But you're contradicting yourselves," Lori said. "Seceding requires the same supermajority."

"Yes, but we believe that the Republicans would actually vote *for* it. Most of them," Franklin said. "They'd see it as removing the primary counterweight to their agenda. So no, they wouldn't vote to get rid of the Electoral College, given that reduces their leverage. But letting California go gives the GOP far *more* power."

"They really don't like us," Calla said. "You should see what I see online."

"Some of these leaders they elect..." Cole said. "The current Speaker of the House thinks Noah's ark was real. That the world is six thousand years old."

"No he does not," Calla said.

"Good segue. What about water?" Oisín asked. "Most of what California uses is from the Colorado River. Which starts in Colorado."

"We could buy water," Daniel said. "Make an arrangement with Colorado and the feds. Or there's the Sierras—billions of liters in snowpack every year. And then there's Mammoth for SoCal. There are so many options."

"What's the feds' incentive to make a deal on water?" Lori asked.

"Food," Daniel answered. "We're the largest agricultural state by a mile. Ninth-largest agricultural economy in the world. Everything grows here, and they need the food we grow."

"There's also desalinization," Franklin added.

"We do have eight hundred miles of coastline," Daniel said.

"Twelve hundred and fifty *kilometers* of coastline. After we switch to the metric system," Cole said.

"Right, right. We could do that," Franklin said. "Face it, we'd look more to Europe than to much of the US. We'd go metric, and we'd be able to enact every rational policy that's currently held back by the regressive states."

"We could join the EU," Cole noted.

"We could," Edie said. "And we should." Lori scoffed and Edie turned to her sister. "Lori, we're in an actual abusive relationship. With a rapist. Whose best friend is a Nazi. Seventy-six million people voted for the rapist-Nazi combo. Staying with these lunatics makes no sense. It's based on sentiment or cowardice or both."

"It'd be cool to make a new flag," Cole said, and half the adults in the audience silently remembered that Cole still played with Legos. Hadn't he auditioned for *Lego Masters*? "And new money."

"I'd want the kind with the little plastic window," Calla said. "Isn't there some country that has money like that?"

"New Zealand," Torin said.

"Again with New Zealand," Oisín said.

"I say we make it oversized, too," Calla said.

"But then we'd all need oversized wallets," Oisín noted. "Then oversized pockets for the oversized wallets. Then oversized pants to accommodate these enormous pockets. It's a lot to think about." Calla and Torin looked to him, unsure if he was joking.

"Don't listen to him, kids," Patrick said. "But do we really need new money? Wouldn't it be easier to use U.S. dollars?"

"Cuba does," Cole said.

"Bad example," Patrick noted.

"Our position is that we'd want our own currency," Franklin said. "We don't want our economy tied to the rise and fall of the U.S. dollar. Especially if we have no say in how they run their Treasury."

"I'm out," Edie said, holding an empty pitcher high. "Should I make more?" No one answered. "I'll make more."

"What about the rest of the blue states?" Lori asked.

Daniel sighed. "It might be a tough road for them."

Lori laughed. "A tough road? What's left of the country would be a permanent Republican stronghold. Without California, there couldn't possibly be another Democratic president. No power in Congress, either."

"That's not necessarily true," Franklin said. "The Dems would have to make some adjustments, and actually address their policies better to the working class. Then they could win. I personally believe Bernie could have beaten Trump."

Cole nodded vigorously.

"If we leave the union, the Northeast leaves next," Patrick pointed out.

"Right. They'd have to do the same thing," Lori said. "They'd have no choice. Maybe Illinois and Colorado and Minnesota, too."

"I see nothing wrong with that," Edie said. She was back, squeezing lemons. "I like it. Three countries. California, New England with whoever else, and then Trumpland. Everyone's with who they want to be with. Three saucy singles instead of an unhappily married throuple."

"I see this like Brexit," Lori said. "A lot of buyer's remorse. Tariffs, trade wars, so many complications. Twenty years of painful adjustments."

"Just the opposite, Lore," Patrick said. "Everything gets simpler. As is, this country is like this giant old house full of rats and garbage and ghosts. We'd be moving into something new and clean."

"We'd trade with the US, just as we would with Canada, Mexico, China, Japan," Franklin said. "It would be quite friendly. Like the U.S. relationship with England is now."

"Or was, until a few months ago," Patrick said.

"It's good to remember the former Soviet Union," Daniel said. "When that broke up in '91, you had a lot of hand-wringing about whether these countries could stand on their own, would there be border skirmishes, would there be chaos… But it was almost entirely peaceful. And everyone's happy."

"Everyone's happy?" Oisín said. "Have you been to the Baltics? No one's happy there."

"But was anyone ever happy in the Baltics?" Patrick asked. No one knew.

"We'd have new passports!" Calla said.

"And if someone from Nevada wanted to come live here, then what?" Edie asked.

"Americans would have the inside track to becoming California citizens," Franklin said. "But it would be a process. Just like if one of us wanted to move to Canada."

"Progressives from elsewhere could come here, and the regressive people could leave," Cole said. "A million would leave us, a few million would move in."

"More than a few million. We'd be inundated," Edie said. "Free health care and lower taxes and no assault weapons killing our kids?"

"And the weather!" Patrick said. "And the time zone."

"Don't say it, Dad," Lori warned.

"Always more time here," Patrick said loudly.

"Back to immigration," Lori said. "My clients are hiding in churches now. They're not showing up to work. And what about the Dreamers?"

"We instantly make the Dreamers citizens," Franklin said. "They're Americans, after all. They've been here all their lives."

"Good," Lori said, her arms crossed over her chest. Edie took note—Lori was softening.

"They'd be called Californians," Edie said. "We're Californians, right? Because we're no longer Americans."

"We naturalize the temporary protected status folks, too," Franklin said. "The Venezuelans and

Salvadorans. That's about sixty-seven thousand in California. That's Day One. After that, though, the border policy has to be rational and organized. I mean, most people just want a *system*. Among immigrant voters that number actually goes up. System, system, system. That's what everyone wants."

Edie looked at her sister and knew Lori was coming around. Lori had been representing immigrants for twenty-two years, and had come to believe that any period when the border was chaotic, or *seemed* chaotic, led to tidal Republican wins all over the country. The key was an orderly border that recognized our need for immigrants, recognized the plight of asylum seekers, but also observed an orderly queue. No one could argue with an orderly queue.

Lori let her mind wander to a preposterous idea: that if California had its own national borders they could maintain a better system, free from GOP xenophobia, its whims and panic. She laughed to herself, realizing all at once that the movement's only hope would be if Katherine was its public face. And she and Lori could run the campaign. They could improve it and professionalize what these oddballs Franklin and Daniel began.

But would a former senator, who had championed the rule of law for decades, come within a thousand miles of an independence movement? Katherine had been determined not to meet these two envoys. She didn't want them to have a picture or an anecdote.

"So what do you want from us?" Oisín said. His sunglasses were back on the bridge of his nose and his posture had returned to that of napping.

"Excuse me?" Franklin asked.

"Action items," Oisín said. "We've heard the talk, now what do you want us to *do*?"

"They wanted Katherine here," Cole said. "Right?"

"Well, sure," Franklin said. "It'd be helpful to have an esteemed former senator on the team. But we need you all to talk it up, we need volunteers, we need—"

"Money," Oisín said. "A lot of money to get a prop on the ballot."

Franklin looked at the fruit at his feet and frowned. "Yes, sure. But we're not really in the fund-raising mode. We're actually not good at fundraising—the two of us aren't at least."

"But you'll accept a donation?" Oisín asked.

"You're ready to donate, kid brother?" Patrick said.

"I like it," Oisín said. "I'll write a check. You take a check?"

"Sure," Franklin said.

Oisín patted his pockets. It was unclear if he really thought he might have brought a checkbook with him. "I don't have it. My brother in the top tax bracket will cover me. You in, Paddy?"

"I'm the one who *called* this meeting," Patrick said. "Of course I'm in."

Edie had spotted Katherine in the kitchen. She leaned over to Lori. "There she is," she whispered.

Katherine was fifty yards away, peeking from behind a linen curtain. Edie caught her eye. Katherine tapped her wrist and turned her hand up, as if to say, "How long will this be going on?"

"I need to talk to her," Edie said, and stood up. *Excuse me*, she mouthed to Franklin and Daniel as she stepped between the mismatched chairs and remnants of fruit.

"Wait, I'm coming too," Lori whispered, and followed Edie into the house.

Katherine had the fridge open. "How long till they're gone?" she asked. She was wearing shorts and sandals and a white Hastings School of Law hoodie. "They look like guys selling Moody Blues records at a flea market."

"I know, I know," Edie said. "But the plan is startlingly rational."

"The secession plan? Are you stoned?" Katherine asked. She turned to Lori. "Don't tell me you're one of them now."

"I thought it was insanity, too," Lori said. "Now the idea of *staying* seems insane. We're married to seventy-seven million maniacs who re-elected a rapist who tried to overthrow the country. This is when historical schisms happen, Kath. How much crazier does it need to get?"

"Lori," Katherine said. "Compare this to the war in Iraq. W is a cuddly elder statesman now, but don't forget he started two wars that killed a million people. By comparison, this is small beans."

"And the attempted coup?" Edie said.

"Outrageous. Catastrophic," Katherine said. "But here we are. We survived. The country survived. A thousand of those people went to jail."

"And now they're all out," Lori said.

"Pardoned by the architect of the coup," Edie said. "And now he's dismantling the entire government."

"So wait four years," Katherine said. She had found a very small watermelon and cut it in half. "It might not even be four years," she said. "Trump will die in office. Mark my words. He's very old, and very unhealthy." She looked out the window again. "Why's the one guy wearing basketball shorts?"

Edie opened the fridge. "He said he was from Concord."

Katherine winced. "They don't wear pants in Concord?"

"Our point is," Lori said, "that these two guys should not lead this movement. They should be hidden away in some research room."

"And you want me to be the public face. No chance."

"Hear us out. Just close your eyes," Edie said.

"I'm not closing my eyes. What are you doing, a magic trick?"

"I just have this picture of the three of us working together again," Edie said. "Like your first run for Congress. One last rodeo."

"You liked the rodeo. I never liked the rodeo," Katherine said.

"We had fun," Edie said. "We were good. Everyone said we were good."

"I wouldn't touch this with a mile-long pole," Katherine said. "My entire legacy would be toast."

"Did she just say legacy?" Lori asked.

"You shouldn't use that word, Kath. It's unseemly," Edie said. "And remember you can't just rest on your record. Re-evalulations happen."

Lori wanted to say, too, that there were few glittering highlights to Katherine's twelve years in office. She voted for the Affordable Care Act. She served on committees. She brought some federal money back to the state. But she was more of a uniter than a leader. Her name wasn't on any legislation that anyone remembered. Instead she said, "That Iraq vote when you were in Congress is not aging well."

Katherine's eyes bulged. "You've always had such a nice touch, Lore."

"Sorry," Lori said. "But you know I'm right. You could lead this. It would be an iconic second act."

"I still don't know what you two see in this," Katherine said. "I get why someone like Cole would be aboard. He loves dumb ideas. Did I tell you he cornered me about UFO disclosures last night?"

"That's Cole," Edie said. "This is us."

"I bet he voted for Jill Stein," Katherine said.

"I *know* he voted for Jill Stein," Edie said, and Katherine looked to the ceiling.

"Think of it like this," Lori said. "We create a platform. The anti–Project 2025. Make it practical and applicable to California—a slate of policies that California could enact if we broke off. Call it California Values."

"I hate that name," Katherine said.

"Project 2026," Edie suggested.

"That's worse," Katherine said.

"You could be the public face of it," Edie said, "and maybe play down the actual independence part if you want. Say you're not sure about that, but it should be explored. In the meantime, you can talk about a slate of policies that we can all agree on. That's enough to get the platform on the news, and the six hundred thousand signatures is a cinch. We don't have to think further than that."

"*You* don't have to think further than that. *I* do."

"Fine. Then let's think even further," Lori said. "We're talking about the founding of a country. A far better country. Take what works and press ahead. I was skeptical but I actually do believe it's time. Why not make an indelible mark on history?"

"Jesus Christ."

"New countries form all the time," Edie said. "In this case, it's just lack of imagination that stops us."

"Are these still good?" Katherine asked. She'd found a small crate of brown strawberries in the fridge.

"They're organic, so probably no?" Edie said. Katherine dumped them in the compost.

"What are you doing up there in Grass Valley, anyway?" Lori asked.

"Plenty," Katherine said. "I'm happy. Don't I get a minute to reflect?"

"You've been out of office three years," Lori said. "How long do you need? People will forget you exist."

"Again, Lori, you are all charm. Don't you think, Torin? Do you know we used to call her Pitbull?"

Edie looked to the doorway to find her son. "How long have you been standing there?"

"Just a minute," he said. "But can I talk to you all?"

"Only if you're changing the subject," Katherine said.

"I'm not changing the subject," he said. "Aunt Kath, I think you should do it."

"You too? Did someone spike the lemonade?"

Torin stepped into the room and scooted onto the kitchen counter. Somehow his thoughts of 4.3 years had only made the secessionist presentation more urgent. A nearby sun had not exploded, but still the lesson seemed apt. Why not do monumental things *now*?

"I just wanted to, like, add my voice here, if you're like, getting a sense of how the family feels about this."

Katherine held up her palm. "Tor, stop. I can't take you seriously with all the 'likes.' Talk in a straight line."

"Fine," Torin said. He'd been chastised for this before. He took a moment and talked slowly, deliberately. "Aunt Kath, I listened for an hour to those guys and I expected nothing. Then I got excited about their idea because it's bold and brave and it would actually improve the lives of, like, forty million people. Just like Mom said, leaving is far more rational than staying. It's just sick masochism to stay. Leaving and creating something new is the way of hope. I know Aunt Lori is against this, but I think you could be different."

"Honey," Lori said.

"No, don't. Please, Aunt Lori. Don't kill this. You adults always complain about us not being interested in anything, not having passions, and then one, like, actual inspiring idea comes along, and we *get* inspired, and then you instantly stomp all over it. You have to actually make up your minds. If you want us to be inspired, then inspire us."

"Tor," Lori said.

He'd lowered his head. He assumed he was about to be scolded. "What? Sorry."

"I'm trying to tell you that I'm in," she said. He lifted his eyes enough to catch his aunt walking toward him. She took his head in her hands. "Now we're just working on Katherine."

"Why are you all in the kitchen?" Calla said. "Everyone out there's wondering if someone died in here."

"No one's dead," Katherine said. "But everyone's lost their minds."

"Wait. Are you all trying to talk her into it?" Calla asked. "Aunt Kath, you should. Please do it. I'll be your assistant."

"This has every hallmark of a cult," Katherine said. "And what are you wearing?"

Calla was still wearing her GENITALS T-shirt. "You're only sixty. You can't just wait out the clock," she said.

"Excuse me?" Katherine said. "Take that off. How does she know how old I am?"

"Calla. You're out of line," Lori said. "And cover that shirt up. You can't be part of this if you're dressed like an adolescent."

Calla found an apron draped over a chair and put it on. The words KITCH BITCH were printed across it.

The aunts gave up.

"What else are you doing these days, Aunt Kath?" Calla asked. "Writing another Washington memoir?"

Katherine leaned her head back and dropped a handful of blueberries into her mouth. "Lori, is your daughter really talking to me this way?"

"Calla," Lori said sternly.

"Sorry," she said, and looked at Katherine and smiled apologetically. "I just don't want you to do that thing where you all paint a picture of something actually beautiful and great, then act like it's a dumb nothing. Or that it's unfeasible and not worth trying."

"It *is* unfeasible," Katherine said. "In a thousand ways it's unfeasible. We could spend the next three years on it, and millions of dollars, and we'd get almost nowhere."

"We could get on the ballot," Edie said.

"Yes. We could," Katherine said. "Lots of idiotic things end up on the ballot. Last year a guy got enough signatures for a proposition that would free all the chickens in the state."

"I voted for that," Calla said.

"Of course you did," Katherine said. "So we'd get on the ballot and it would get about thirty percent of the vote, because every dumb proposition gets thirty percent. Then what? We've spent tens of millions of dollars and thousands of hours only to be embarrassed and with nothing to show for it."

"But if *you* did it, it'd be different," Calla said. "You could explain it to people. The reason those other measures don't pass is because they don't have a two-term senator and feminist icon behind it. People trust you."

Katherine turned to Edie. "Listen to this one. Did you coach her?"

"I didn't talk to her. I've been in here with *you*," Edie said, and looked out the window. Franklin and Daniel seemed to be lost. Their presentation had ended, Oisín appeared to be asleep, and Paolo had begun piling fruit on Franklin's lap. "I better get back out there," she said, and returned to the patio.

Lori took Katherine's hand. "Can we walk? Kids, we'll be back."

They left the kitchen and took the stone-step path through more cherry blossoms that no one could remember planting.

Lori picked a pink-white blossom. "Would you consider doing this for Edie?"

"Running a fringe campaign? As a favor?"

"I think Edie needs it. When her kids are at school she goes to see movies alone. She brings a thermos, if you know what I mean. She needs some kind of purpose."

"*She's* welcome to do this!" Katherine said, and stopped, her arms stiff and gesticulating all over the dappled light. "That's what you both are missing. And your Lady Macbeth kids! They are scary, Lori! You're all welcome to do this without me."

"I think you need it, too," Lori said evenly. "You're so young. Senators fade quickly. You want to start teaching the occasional course at UC Davis? Are you the adjunct type? You want to grade papers written by kids who didn't want to write them?"

"What do you want me to say? Yes, I want to grade those fucking papers. More than I want to do another campaign. I haven't worn heels in six months and I don't plan to do that again till one of those kids gets married."

"I think you should do this."

"No."

"You mean yes," Lori said. "In this state we say yes."

"No."

Katherine sat down on the buffalo grass Edie had planted under the apricots. Lori sat across from her. They were cross-legged, their backs rigid, eye to eye.

"You're only sixty," Lori said. "You have so much time."

"No."

"There's always more time in California."

"You're such an idiot."

"I think I'm hearing you say yes."

Katherine looked over Lori's shoulder, at Torin and Calla, who were watching from the kitchen window. The funny thing was that Katherine had thought seriously about secession all the way back in 2000, before she'd run for Congress. When five men on the Supreme Court gave the election to Bush, she thought the republic had pivoted, hard, to something different from a democracy. Then there were the wars, the school shootings, the hyperviolence made possible by an increasingly unregulated gun market, the climate change denial, the shredding of the social safety net, the skyrocketing health care prices, an attempted and forgotten coup—all the relentless chaos of Republican rule. And now the cycle was complete. The U.S. was an oligarchy-in-training, a kind of fawning kid brother to Russia, a kleptocracy whose wealth—most of it, anyway, a criminal percentage of it—was in the hands of a handful of selfish men. And these men controlled a government that was determined not to benefit anyone in any way. It was time to split off and start over.

"And when they outlaw abortion, we need to be apart," Lori said.

Katherine looked at her sister and wanted to say, *Of course I want a new nation. But I'm tired. And I don't want to look foolish. And did I mention I'm tired?*

Instead she said, "I'm not saying yes."

Lori leaned in and hugged her. "Your words are saying no, but your eyes are saying, 'Yes, yes, we must, let's three sisters do this! Because only we can! Yes! Yes! Yes!"

"No."

"This'll be fun," Lori said. "You'll be Joan of Arc."

"Please no."

"Susan B. Anthony."

"That's better."

"No one remembers the cautious and weak," Lori said.

"You need to stop."

"I'll stop."

Katherine fell back onto the plush grass and looked at the satin sky through the gaps in the trees. "I do want to be near you and Edie," she said.

"Right," Lori said. "You can."

"I'm realizing that I've been lonely," Katherine said.

"Good," Lori said. "Sorry. You know what I mean. We'll fix that."

"I'll do it for you two first," she said. "California second."

"That's fine," Lori said. "For me, it's the other way around, but we don't have to quibble. We'll figure it out. You know what they say—"

"Don't say it. Don't you dare say it."

"There's always more time— "

"Stop. Don't."

"But you know it's true."

"I do know," Katherine said. "You know I do. I really do."

"I think we could actually do this."

"God help us. I do, too."

DAVE EGGERS is the author of many books, including *The Monk of Mokha*, *The Circle*, *Heroes of the Frontier*, and *A Hologram for the King*. In 2024, his all-ages novel *The Eyes & the Impossible* won the Newbery Medal.

NOTES & ACKNOWLEDGMENTS

The author would like to thank Emilio Garcia-Ruiz, Alex Fong, Ron Kitagawa, and everyone at the *San Francisco Chronicle*, who kindly published this in a Sunday edition of the paper. Thanks also to Amanda Uhle, Annie Dills, Conor O'Brien, India Claudy, Caitlin Van Dusen, Michael Lewis, Tom Barbash, and Peter Orner.

Uncle Patrick's Secessionist Breakfast is the eighth story in *The Forgetters* series of mini-books. If all goes according to plan, these stand-alone stories will someday be part of a larger work. Exactly when this will happen, no one can be sure.

BOOKS IN THE FORGETTERS SERIES

The Museum of Rain

Oisín Mahoney is an American Army vet in his seventies who is asked to lead a group of young grand-nieces and grand-nephews on a walk through the hills of California's Central Coast. Their destination is a place called the Museum of Rain, which may or may not still exist. A testament to family, memory, and what we leave behind. *Also check out the audio version, narrated by Jeff Daniels.*

The Honor of Your Presence

Winner of a 2024 O. Henry Award

A homebody niece and her adventurous, almost-British uncle begin to attend parties to which they are not invited—an innocuous lark that becomes a very funny and lyrical referendum on why humans congregate and celebrate. Named a Distinguished Story in *The Best American Short Stories*.

The Comebacker

In this comic, lyrical story, Lionel is a beat reporter covering the San Francisco Giants. When a new pitcher is brought up from the minor leagues, he shows Lionel a rare, even unprecedented, ability to see the beauty in the game he's paid to play.

The Keeper of the Ornaments

Cole lives alone, has no pets, and has grown accustomed to a home life of profound quiet (not to say tedium). When a raucous household moves into the apartment next door, Cole assumes he'll have to move. But his new neighbors, and their very odd cats, see him differently than he sees himself. A powerful meditation on forgiveness, grace, and the happiness of being called upon.

Where the Candles Are Kept

Two seemingly sullen California teenagers are sent to visit their uncle Oisín in rural Idaho one summer, and ponder their escape soon after they land. In this wry and suspenseful story, all three are forced to decide who and what they care about, and if they have any role in the saving of a life.

The Ocean Is Everyone's but It Is Not Yours

Aurora Mahoney runs one of three vaguely competitive whale-watching businesses on the Monterey coast. It's a life of great beauty, wonder and camaraderie, but after one of her fellow captains retires, a new, and decidedly different, sort of captain takes his place. What had been a simple and charmed life is clouded by a sinister, and yet aloof, new force on the waterfront. A page-turning examination of what makes a paradise, and how easily one human can destroy it.

Sanrevelle

Winner of a 2025 O. Henry Award

A man named Hop, not too young and not too old, lives in a sinking skyscraper and works for a personal-injury lawyer who's slowly losing his mind. Every day Hop stares out at the tiny boats on the San Francisco Bay, wanting to be out there and not filing paperwork for a cloistered madman. Finally Hop goes to a rickety dock by the sea, seeking sailing lessons. He meets the singular Sanrevelle, a barefoot captain, who leads him out of a grievance-based existence and into a life of speed and cold and light.

Author proceeds from this book go to McSweeney's Literary Arts Fund, helping to ensure the survival of nonprofit independent publishing.

www.mcsweeneys.net

McSweeney's, founded in 1998, amplifies original voices and pursues the most ambitious literary projects.

WE PUBLISH:

McSweeney's Quarterly Concern, a journal of new writing
The Believer magazine, featuring essays, interviews, and columns
Illustoria, an art and storytelling magazine for young readers
McSweeneys.net, a daily humor website.

An intrepid list of fiction, nonfiction, poetry, art and uncategorizable books, including the Of the Diaspora series—important works of twentieth-century literature by Black American writers.